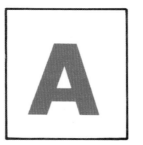  

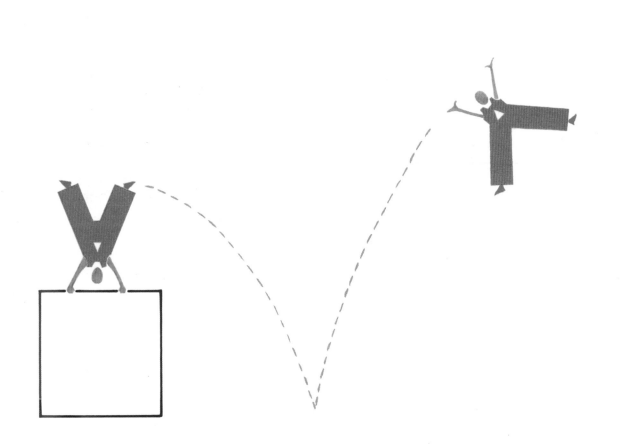

ALPHABATICS

Suse MacDonald

Aladdin Paperbacks
New York London Toronto Sydney

Aa

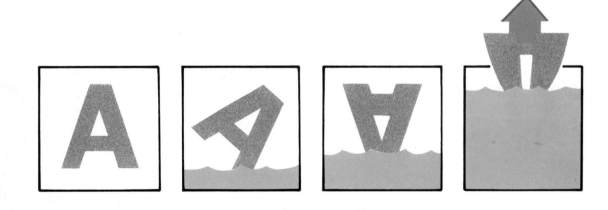

Ark

Bb

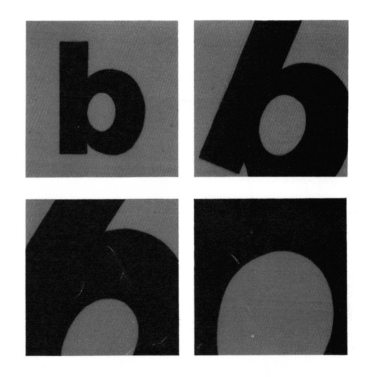

balloon

Cc

Clown

Dd

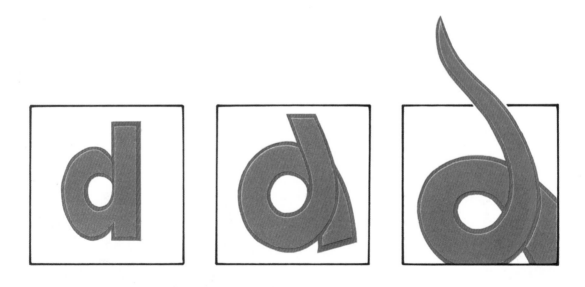

dragon

Ee

Elephant

Ff

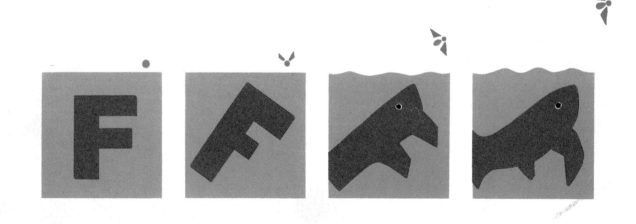

Fish

Gg

Giraffe

Hh

h

house

insect

Jj

**jack-
in-the-box**

Kk

Kite

Ll

Lion

Mm

mustache

Nn

nest

Oo

owl

Plane

Qq

Quail

Rr

 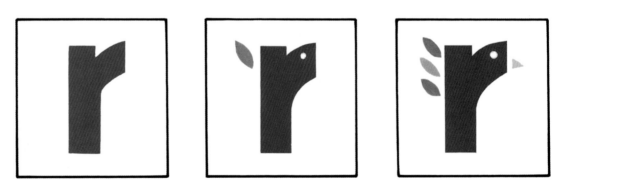 

rooster

Ss

Swan

Tt

Tree

Uu

umbrella

Vv

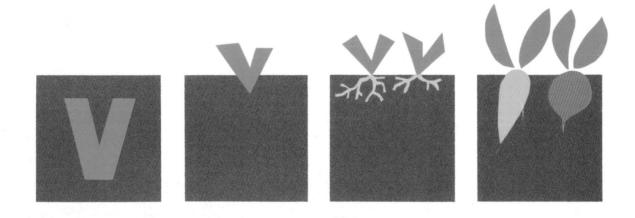

Vegetables

Ww

Whale

Xx

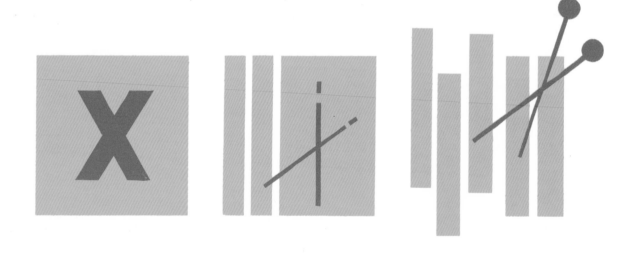

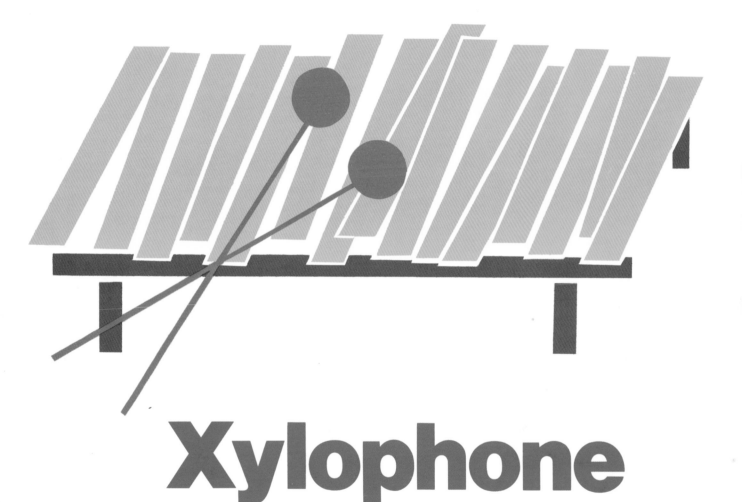

Xylophone

Yy

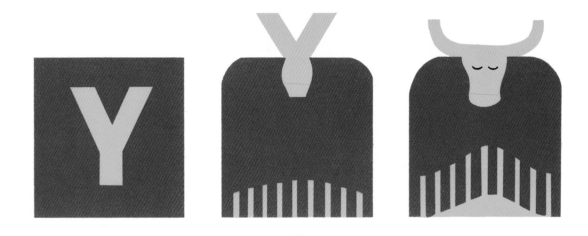

Yak

Zz

Zebra

For Stuart, with special thanks to Susan and Deborah

ALADDIN PAPERBACKS. An imprint of Simon & Schuster Children's Publishing Division. 1230 Avenue of the Americas, New York, NY 10020. Copyright © 1986 by Suse MacDonald. All rights reserved, including the right of reproduction in whole or in part in any form. ALADDIN PAPERBACKS and colophon are registered trademarks of Simon & Schuster, Inc. Also available in a Simon & Schuster Books for Young Readers hardcover edition. Manufactured in the United States of America. First Aladdin Paperbacks edition 1992. Second Aladdin Paperbacks edition June 2005. 10 9 8 7 6 5 4 3 2 1

The Library of Congress has cataloged the first paperback edition as follows: MacDonald, Suse. Alphabatics / by Suse MacDonald.—1st Aladdin Books ed. p. cm. Originally published: New York: Bradbury Press, 1986. Summary: The letters of the alphabet are transformed and incorporated into twenty-six illustrations, so that the hole in "b" becomes a balloon and "y" turns into the head of a yak. ISBN 0-689-71625-7 (1st Aladdin pbk.) 1. English Language—Alphabet—Juvenile literature. [1. Alphabet.] I. Title   PE1155.M3   1992   [E]—dc20   91-38497   ISBN 1-4169-0305-4 (2nd Aladdin pbk.)